DATE DUE			
SEP 2 3 2006			
2/24			

THE LITTLE RED ENGINE AND THE ROCKET

Pictures by
Leslie Wood

Story by
Diana Ross

ANDRE DEUTSCH
CLASSICS

First published in Great Britain in 1956 by Faber and Faber Ltd.

This edition published in 1999 by André Deutsch Classics.

ISBN 0 233 99405 X.

The Baronet was waiting on the station at Callington.

"I want to go to Taddlecombe to catch the London train. There's a meeting of scientists at the Royal Society."

"What is a scientist?" said the Little Red Engine.

An earwig on the signal box gave him the answer.

"A scientist is a man who finds out about the world. The Baronet's a scientist. He learns about earthworms. They say he's a World Authority."

"Oh!" said the Little Red Engine. "I feel honoured to serve him. I had better hurry up and catch the London train. WHOOOOOOOO."

At Seven Sisters the schoolmaster was waiting. His name was John Trim, but in spite of his name he was always untidy.

"I want to go to Taddlecombe to catch the London train. There's a meeting of Inventors at the Royal Society."

"What is an inventor?" asked the Little Red Engine.

A starling on the telegraph wires gave him the answer.

"An inventor is a man who finds new ways of doing things. John

Trim is inventing a wonderful machine. It's for counting chickens before they are hatched. He says he'll be world famous as soon as it's finished."

"Oh!" said the Little Red Engine. "I feel honoured to serve him. I had better hurry up and catch the London train. WHOOOOOOOO."

So the Little Red Engine went quickly and it caught the London train.

When they got to the meeting in London, John Trim and the Baronet were just in time for the speeches.

The Cleverest Scientist of all got up. He was an Astronomer, a man who studies the stars.

"Above the earth is air," he said. "Above the air is Space. In Space there are the sun and the moon, the planets and the stars. We can see them through our telescopes and learn a lot about them. But if we could go into Space we could learn a lot more. Surely the Inventors can help us to get there?"

The Cleverest Inventor got up and said, "If you throw a stone up in the air it will fall back to earth when the force of the throw is spent. The

earth's attraction pulls it back. We call it the pull of gravity.

"If you want to travel in space you must go in a rocket so fast and so far that you go beyond the pull of the earth's attraction. We must get away from gravity. It could be done if we set our minds to it."

A very Cautious Inventor said, "Let us make this rocket secretly. If people find out what we're doing they may copy us or laugh at us. Let us build it in a country place, remote and quiet."

"Not too remote and quiet," said a very Practical Scientist, "or what about supplies? You can't make a rocket out of country produce."

The Baronet jumped up. He was very excited.

"I know the very place! The district I live in! It is quiet and remote but served by an admirable railway."

"The Little Red Engine, they call it," cried John Trim beside him. "A truly admirable railway. It will bring you all you need."

"The thing shall be done," said the Scientists and Inventors. "The

Experimental Station shall be somewhere near Taddlecombe. From there we will send our first rocket into Space."

The meeting broke up in great excitement.

When the people of Taddlecombe heard of it they, too, were excited. They held a mass meeting in the square on market day.

"Down with the Scientists! Down with the Inventors!" cried all the people. "Rockets! Spaceships! Experimental Stations! We don't hold with such things! We prefer things as they are! We'll protest to the Government. We want to be left alone!"

But Tom Perry, the gamekeeper's eldest, and one of John Trim's best pupils got up and said, "We young chaps think different. We likes the idea. Liven up the ol' place. And instead o' leaving home to find work in the towns we can all bide at home and get work at the Station."

"That's true," said the mothers and at once changed their minds, and they spoke to the fathers and they changed their minds, and as most of the people were parents or young folk, suddenly the crowd

seemed all in favour of it.

"We should move with the times," they said to each other.

"'Tis an up and coming place, our Taddlecombe. We believe in progress."

And they all went home.

As the porters and the engine drivers talked it over, the engines overheard and were very disgusted.

"We have too much to do as it is," said Pride o' the North, "without the extra freight they'll expect us to carry."

"Going into Space! The very idea!" snorted Beauty of the South. "As if my Summer Excursions weren't good enough!"

But the Little Red Engine was happy.

"WHOOOOO, WHOOOOOOOO," it cried. "We're going to build a rocket to go into Space. The first that's ever done it. And they need my help to do it. How busy I shall be, and I love to be busy! WHOOOOOOOO!"

On Monday morning at Taddlecombe Junction a group of Surveyors stood on the platform with their sextants, theodolites and chains.

"We must go to Seven Sisters to survey the land," they said. "You cannot build anything till that has been settled. We think the place is suitable. Where is the train?"

"Here is the train," said the Little Red Engine, "In you get and away we go. WHOOOOOOOO."

And every morning for a week the Little Red Engine took the Surveyors to Seven Sisters with their sextants, theodolites and chains, and back again in the evening.

The next Monday morning at Taddlecombe Junction a group of Architects stood on the platform with their ground plans, set squares, callipers and rulers.

"We have got out plans for an Engineering Workshop, and in that we will make the rocket; for an Atomic Pile to breed the power to drive it, and a Launching Platform from which to send it off. We must go to the site and check up on the drawings. Where is the train?"

"Here is the train," said the Little Red Engine. "In you get and away we go. WHOOOOOOOO."

And every morning for a week the Little Red Engine took the Architects to Seven Sisters with their ground plans, set squares, callipers and rulers, and home again in the evening.

The next Monday morning at Taddlecombe Junction, on every siding were wagons and trucks.

Wagons of timber.

Wagons of brick.

Wagons of sand and cement.

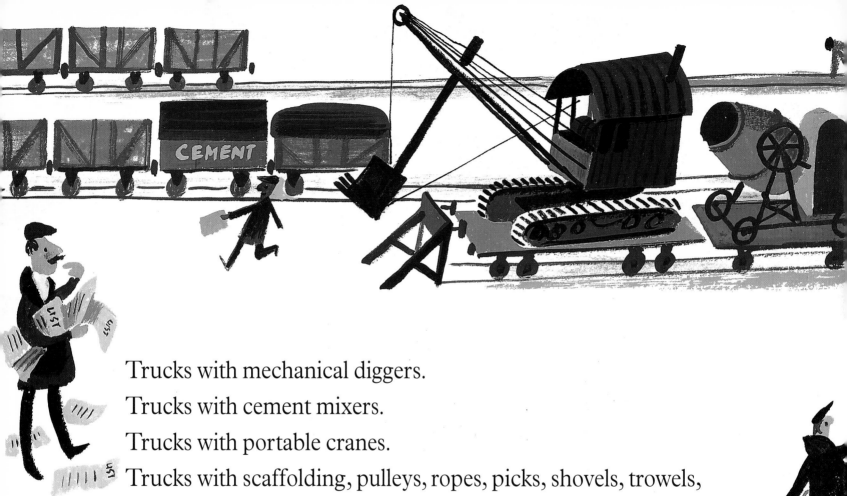

Trucks with mechanical diggers.

Trucks with cement mixers.

Trucks with portable cranes.

Trucks with scaffolding, pulleys, ropes, picks, shovels, trowels, hammers and nails.

A Quantity Surveyor stood on the platform with a huge sheaf of papers under his arm.

"I have all the orders, specifications and invoices," he said,

"For all the materials for the Experimental Station. Where is the train?"

"Here is the train," said the Little Red Engine. "In you get and away we go. WHOOOOOOOO."

And every morning for three weeks the Little Red Engine took wagons and trucks of material along the line to Seven Sisters and brought them back empty in the evening. The next Monday morning at Taddlecombe Junction was a Building Contractor with his

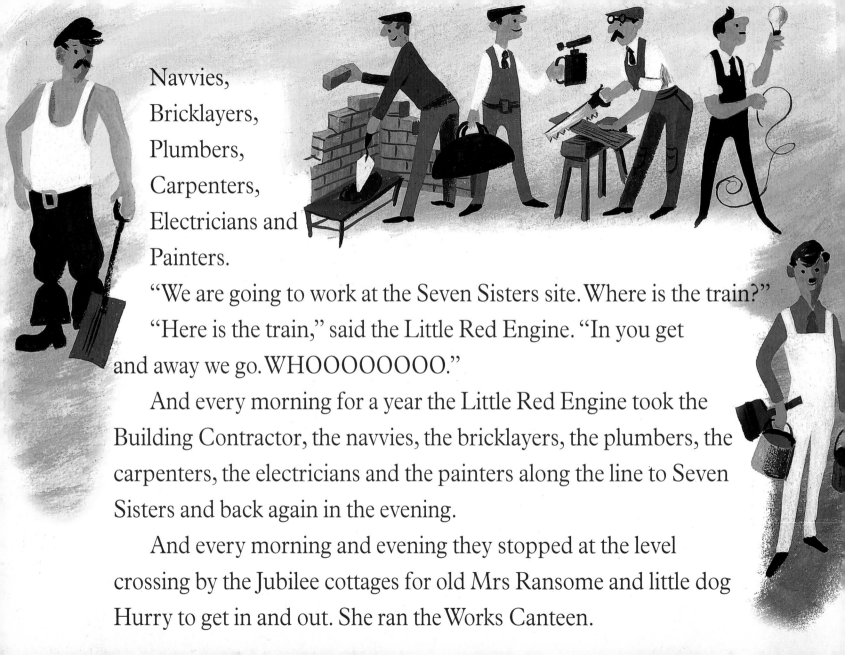

Navvies,
Bricklayers,
Plumbers,
Carpenters,
Electricians and
Painters.

"We are going to work at the Seven Sisters site. Where is the train?"

"Here is the train," said the Little Red Engine. "In you get and away we go. WHOOOOOOOO."

And every morning for a year the Little Red Engine took the Building Contractor, the navvies, the bricklayers, the plumbers, the carpenters, the electricians and the painters along the line to Seven Sisters and back again in the evening.

And every morning and evening they stopped at the level crossing by the Jubilee cottages for old Mrs Ransome and little dog Hurry to get in and out. She ran the Works Canteen.

"Most important person on the site, I am," she'd say. "What would the poor boys do without their cup o' tea?"

So the navvies dug the foundations and put up the scaffolding, the bricklayers put up the walls, the plumbers put in the pipes and drains, the carpenters fitted the roof beams, the windows, the floors and the doors, and the electricians did the wiring, and the painters finished everything off with two coats of Fine Gloss Emulsion Paint, blue and white.

And then the buildings were ready.

So the next Monday morning at Taddlecombe Junction a group of Mechanics stood on the platform with their spanners, ratchets and oil cans, and in the sidings were a hundred trucks of machinery; boilers, furnaces, turbines, pistons, dynamos and converters.

"We have come to install the machinery for the Engineering workshop, the Atomic Pile, and the Launching Platform. Where is the train?"

"Here is the train," said the Little Red Engine. "In you get and away we go. WHOOOOOOOO."

And every day for a month it took the Mechanics with their spanners, ratchets and oil cans along the line to Seven Sisters and home again in the evening.

And then the place was in working order.

The next Monday morning at Taddlecombe Junction were the Mayor and Corporation, the Surveyors, Architects and Contractors, the Mechanics and all the people who had worked on the buildings, not forgetting old Mrs Ransome and little dog Hurry.

And they were all in their best clothes, including little dog Hurry.

"His Worship the Mayor will open the Experimental Station. Where is the train?"

"Here is the train," said the Little Red Engine. "In you get and away we go. WHOOOOOOOO."

On reaching Seven Sisters they gathered in the workshop. The Mayor made a speech, and pulled a little lever and all the machinery went into production.

Then they left "Sleepy" Hawkins, the night watchman in charge and they all went back to a banquet at Taddlecombe Town Hall.

The very next morning on Taddlecombe platform stood the Cleverest Scientist with his logarithms and calculus, and the Cleverest Inventor with his blueprints and models, and Consulting Engineers with their jigs, micrometers and gauges, and an office staff of Clerks and Typists, and Personnel Managers, Shop Stewards and Workmen.

"We have come to start work on building the rocket. Where is the train?"

"Here is the train," said the Little Red Engine. "In you get and away we go. WHOOOOOOOO."

And every morning for five years the Little Red Engine took the Cleverest Scientist and the Cleverest Inventor, the Consulting Engineers and the Clerks and the Typists, the Personnel Managers, Shop Stewards and Workmen along the line to Seven Sisters and home again in the evening.

And they still stopped for old Mrs Ransome and little dog Hurry, for they, too, could not get on without their cup of tea.

At the end of that time the rocket was ready. It was made of Super-High-Tension-Non-Magnetic Alloy. There was a pressurized cabin where the passengers would be, and a separate compartment for the atomic powered dynamos. It had three booster-rockets to send it on its way, retractable wings for descent, and mobile fins for navigation.

It was finished off with Infra-Red Absorbent crimson paint which was considered the best colour to withstand the cosmic rays met with in space, which are very much stronger than sun rays.

Everyone on the site was allowed to go in and see it.

"Why, 'tis a little Red Rocket to go with our Little Red Engine," said old Mrs Ransome, when she saw it with her little dog Hurry. "Fancy that."

"Tomorrow we have a trial," said the Cleverest Inventor, "and for that I would like some animals. If we see the effect of space on an animal's smaller body we can guess the effect it may produce on man. I suppose your little

dog Hurry would not be a volunteer?"

"I'd be proud to volunteer," said little dog Hurry, "but would I be allowed a friend to go with me?"

"As many as you like," said the Cleverest Inventor. "Allow me to congratulate you on your adventurous spirit."

The very next morning, little dog Hurry was ready with the gamekeeper's cat from Seldom Spinney and six of the frogs from Noman's Puddle.

"Though we're going into Space we must start in the Little Red Engine. I hope it isn't late," said little dog Hurry.

"Here I am," said the Little Red Engine. "In you get and away we go. WHOOOOOOOO."

When they came to the launching platform at Merryman's Rising the Cleverest Inventor was surprised and delighted.

"So many volunteers is very encouraging," he said.

So they all got in the rocket and the doors were shut, a lever was pulled, and in a flash of fire, a WHOOOOOSH and a ROAR the rocket went up.

"WHOOOOOOOOOOO, Bon Voyage," cried the Little Red Engine, watching from the line.

The rocket came down at ten o'clock the next morning as the Little Red Engine pulled in at Merryman's Rising.

The doors of the rocket were opened. Out came the volunteers.

"Well, what was it like?" cried the Little Red Engine.

"What was it like?" echoed all the people.

"It felt a bit funny at first," said little dog Hurry, jumping at old Mrs Ransome and licking her hand. "As we gathered speed we felt squeezed like an orange. But very soon that finished and the end was delightful. We felt ourselves grow light, and we floated about like fairies, very peculiar and surprising."

"That happens in Space," said the Cleverest Scientist. "They call it Free Fall. It must feel peculiar."

"It didn't worry us," said the frogs, "we are used to floating round in the water." They rather liked pretending that nothing surprised them.

"And I had nine kittens," said the gamekeeper's cat. "I shall call them after the planets, Mercury, Venus, Mars, Jupiter, Saturn, Uranus, Neptune and Pluto. But the extra one I shall call Tish after his father. I suppose it's a record - to be born in space, I mean."

And she carried them very gently in her mouth, out of the rocket to a

quiet place she knew of behind the stove in the First Aid post.

The Cleverest Inventor was delighted with the test.

"You have been into Space with no bad results at all. We will give you each a medal to commemorate the occasion. But we are nine medals short. We weren't expecting the kittens. They shall have a certificate and a place on the Station Staff."

"I will make a note of it," said the Personnel Manager.

"Where you have been today, Man shall go tomorrow," cried the Cleverest Scientist. "I and my friend, the Inventor, must hurry home to prepare for it."

And the very next day at Taddlecome station, WHAT a gathering was there! The Cleverest Scientist and the Cleverest Inventor, the President and all the members of the Royal Society, the King and Queen themselves but coming incognito, the photographers and journalists of all the world's papers, and such a crowd besides to see the first men to go up into Space. Not only the Little Red Engine but Pride o' the North and Beauty of the South were called upon to take them to the launching platform at Merryman's Rising.

When everyone was there, the Cleverest Scientist and the Cleverest Inventor got in the rocket together.

Before he shut the door the Scientist looked out.

"I want to thank all the people who have made this possible, from my friend, the Inventor here, to the frogs and the cat and little dog Hurry, not even forgetting the Little Red Engine. All my life I have wanted to see clearly in Space, and now that I can it's the happiest day of my life."

"It isn't of mine," grumbled Pride o' the North. "I never thought to see the day I'd find myself on a little branch line."

"I said the rocket would upset things," grunted Beauty of the South.

But at that moment, with a FLASH and a WHOOOOSH and a ROAR and a cheer from all the people, the rocket went up.

"There - that's the end of you and me," said Beauty of the South. "They won't be bothered with engines now they've got their rockets and contraptions."

"Indeed, and you're wrong," said the Little Red Engine. "And even if you were right it wouldn't really matter. If I've served my turn that's good enough for me. They've gone into Space and I helped them do it. One good thing leads on to another. That's the way of the world. WHOOOOOOEEEEEE."

And the Little Red Engine looked proudly at the sky where a fine trail of vapour was all that could be seen of the rocket.

THE END